This Little Tiger book belongs to:

Hannah

For Ciara, Gracie, Francesca,
Emilia, Hetty, Freya and Martha
~ HR

For Bernie and Brenda Nicholas
~ MS

LITTLE TIGER PRESS
An imprint of Magi Publications
1 The Coda Centre, 189 Munster Road, London SW6 6AW
www.littletigerpress.com

First published in Great Britain 2007

Text copyright © Hilary Robinson 2007
Illustrations copyright © Mandy Stanley 2007
Hilary Robinson and Mandy Stanley have asserted their rights
to be identified as the author and illustrator of this work under
the Copyright, Designs and Patents Act, 1988

A CIP catalogue record for this book is available from the British Library

Printed in China

2 4 6 8 10 9 7 5 3 1

The Princess's
Secret Sleepover

Hilary Robinson   Mandy Stanley

LITTLE TIGER PRESS
London

I've just been to a sleepover party at my friend Amy's house. Her address is 2 Palace Place. It made me wonder what it's like to sleep in a real palace. I'm going to write to my friend Princess Isabella and ask her.

38 Sunny Close,
Townsville

Dear Princess Isabella
I was wondering what it's
like sleeping in a palace. Do you
have a four-poster bed with
curtains on it and are your
nighties made from silk?
Love Lucy
x   x
x   x   x

Dear Lucy
Princess Isabella has asked me to
write and thank you for your letter.
The Princess's bed does have satin
drapes, and she has lots of silk
nightwear.

But secretly, she prefers to wear . . .

. . . *spotty pyjamas!*

38 Sunny Close,
Townsville

Dear Princess Isabella
Thank you for your letter.
My favourite toy dog, Snuggles,
always comes with me to
sleepovers and sits on my
pillow while I sleep. Can you tell
me do princesses have special
toys to watch over them
at night?

Love Lucy

x x x

Dear Lucy
Princess Isabella has asked me to thank you
for your letter and to say that she is given lots
of beautiful dolls that sit in glass cabinets
in her bedroom.

But secretly, her most
loyal guard and friend is . . .

. . . Trusty!

Dear Lucy
Princess Isabella has asked me to write to say that she
is allowed to stay up late listening to the royal storyteller.

*But secretly, when he's gone
to bed, the royal maids sneak in . . .*

. . . to sing in their girl band,
Isabella and the Dusty Daisies!

38 Sunny Close,
Townsville

Dear Princess Isabella,
Your girl band sounds great.
Amy and I love making friendship
bracelets and braiding each
other's hair before we go to bed.
Do you ever do that?
× Love Lucy × × ×
×
P.S. I'm sending you a
friendship bracelet.

Dear Lucy

Princess Isabella has asked me to write and say thank you for the lovely friendship bracelet. When her cousin Princess Sophia comes to visit, their hair is brushed one hundred times with a silver hairbrush.

But secretly, when no one else is around, they like to do . . .

. . . *face painting!*

Last night I had a great idea for something else we could do at a sleepover. I was so excited that I had to write to Princess Isabella to tell her all about it.

Dear Lucy
The Princess has asked me to write to say
that while many royal princesses do eat banquets
at sleepovers, the Princess and her loyal friend
Trusty prefer midnight feasts. They would be
delighted if, on the Princess's birthday this
year, you might be kind enough to . . .

. . . *join them!*

Enjoy more royal reads from Little Tiger Press!

For information regarding any of the above titles
or for our catalogue, please contact us:
Little Tiger Press, 1 The Coda Centre,
189 Munster Road, London SW6 6AW
Tel: 020 7385 6333 Fax: 020 7385 7333
E-mail: info@littletiger.co.uk
www.littletigerpress.com